Getting Used to Harry

by
Cari Best

with pictures by
Diane Palmisciano

Orchard Books ~ New York

For Al—wherever you are—C.B.

For my father—D.P.

Text copyright © 1996 by Cari Best

Illustrations copyright © 1996 by Diane Palmisciano

Orchard Books
95 Madison Avenue
New York, NY 10016

Manufactured in the United States of America
Printed by Barton Press, Inc.   Bound by Horowitz/Rae
Book design by Chris Hammill Paul

10   9   8   7   6   5   4   3   2   1

The text of this book is set in 15 point ITC Esprit.   The illustrations are oil pastel.

Library of Congress Cataloging-in-Publication Data

Best, Cari.
    Getting used to Harry / by Cari Best ; with pictures by Diane Palmisciano.
        p.   cm.
    "A Melanie Kroupa book"—Half t.p.
    Summary: When her mother marries Harry, Cynthia finds that she has to adjust to changes in her life at home.
    ISBN 0-531-09494-4. — ISBN 0-531-08794-8 (lib. bdg.)
    [1. Family life—Fiction. 2. Fathers and daughters—Fiction. 3. Marbles (Game)—Fiction.] I. Palmisciano, Diane, ill. II. Title.
    PZ7.B46579Ge   1996
    [E]—dc20   95-23176

When Inky, my mother, married
Harry the shoe store man,
there was music and dancing
and kissing and hugging
and laughing and crying.

Dumplings to drop, drinks to drip, and dress-up shoes from Harry's store.

Inky danced with Harry,
Harry danced with me,
I danced with Inky,
and we all danced together.
"Isn't love the berries!"
sang Harry.

Then the music stopped and Inky
said, "I love you, Harry."

And Harry said, "I love you, Inky."

And they both said, "We love you, Cynthia."

But when Inky and Harry toodle-ooed off
to the mountains, I had to go home with
Grandma. "Love is the pits," I told her.

All the time Inky and Harry
were away, Grandma and I
played games.

We even played wedding.
Grandma let me be the bride.
She was the groom. Pansy was Cynthia.
But when I said, "Toodle-oo, Pansy.
Grandma and I are off to the mountains,"
Pansy looked so sad that I came right back.

Soon Inky and Harry came back, too.
They were full of flowers, and red cheeks,
and we-missed-you, Cynthias.

Pansy got so excited when she saw Harry
that she puddled.

Harry got so excited when he saw Pansy
that he sneezed.

Inky sang "I'm Just Wild about Harry,"
and I went to my room to play marbles.

From then on, Harry was everywhere.

Standing   sitting

slipping and sneezing

washing,
whistling

waiting and watching.

Sometimes I wished Harry
would go home.
Then I realized he *was* home.

Before Harry, Inky always had time for barefoot ballet, the Kitchen Sink at Jan's Ice-Cream Parlor, and a peppermint shampoo whenever Pansy started smelling like dog.

After Harry, Pansy and I had to wait while Inky
trimmed Harry's hair, tried on new shoes, and danced
cheeky-cheeky to the music on the radio.

We ended up doing barefoot ballet all by ourselves.
I clapped for Pansy and she clapped for me.

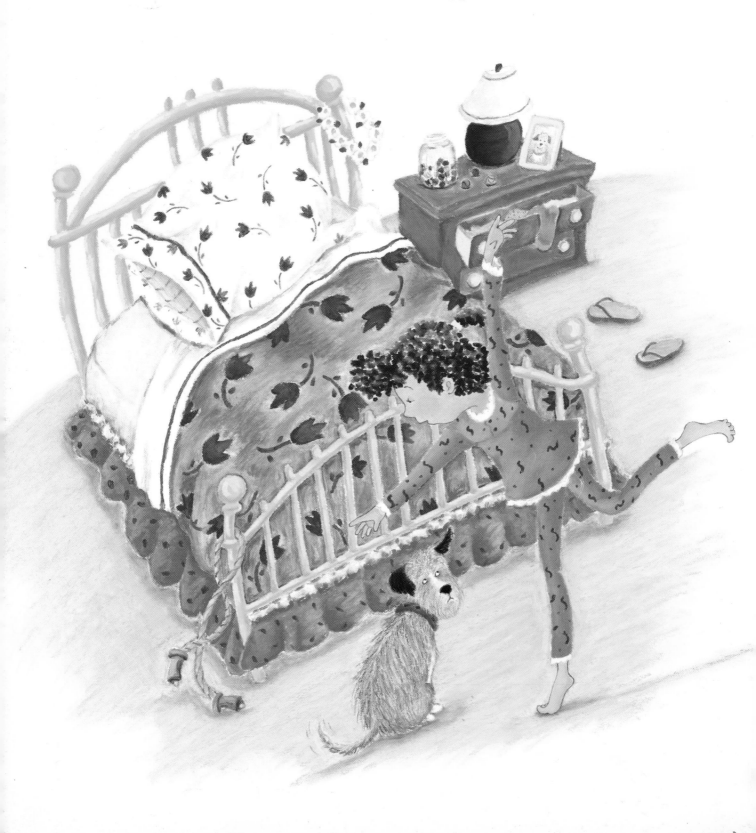

Inky always clapped for Harry whenever he
cooked fancy. Which was every night.
Harry said a good sauce could never have too
much garlic. One night he cooked spaghetti.

"The pasta is perfect," sighed Inky, taking a taste.

"The sauce is superb," sighed Harry, licking his lips.

"The garlic is gross," I sighed, spraying everyone with perfect pasta and superb sauce.

"Whatever happened to pasta plain the way we like it?" I grumbled all the way to my room.

"Harry is coming out of our ears," I told Grandma.

"Now, Cynthia," she said. "It will take a while
for you to get used to Harry. I'm sure he's trying
very hard to get used to you, too."

"Used to me?" I said. "What's there to get used to?"

That night I found out.
I was trying very hard to
fall asleep.

With my blanket.

Without my blanket.

On my side, with my feet on the pillow.

With a bedtime story.

Without a bedtime story.

Shooting imaginary marbles.
Counting my teeth.
Nothing worked.

All I could think about was
how things used to be.

Before Harry.

Finally I got out of bed and
started jumping rope.

All of a sudden I saw a giant shadow. It was Harry!

"Sometimes when I can't sleep," he said, taking the cotton out of his ears, "I count shoes. Like high-tops, Mary Janes, hiking boots, tap shoes, toe shoes, and saddle shoes."

"Who cares about shoes," I said.

"And sometimes when I really can't sleep, I take a flashlight walk," said Harry.

"What's a flashlight walk?" I said. "I'll try anything."

First Harry showed me a big green moth camouflaged on the wall of our house. Then a frog as still as a statue. The night sizzled and buzzed. Acorns fell all around us. I had never been outside in my pajamas before. I kicked the leaves on Peach Street. "Oak, maple, birch, and pine," said Harry, showing me which was which.

When we got to the park, Harry let me hold the flashlight. He found a stick and drew a big circle around us. Something familiar jiggled in his pocket. Marbles! "The secret is backspin," said Harry, the hotshot, spinning his shooter clear across the circle.

Then he let me try.

"I didn't know you collected marbles," I said.

"I knew you did," he said, smiling.

We walked all the way to Ruby Street and stopped right in front of Harry's Shoe Store. Out of the blue Harry asked, "What do you think, Cynth?" like I was his business partner.

I looked from one end of the window to the other. "Boy, could you use some help! Why don't you put the moon boots here, the dress-up shoes here, and the flip-flops here," I said, pointing.

"I didn't know you liked shoes," Harry said.

"I knew you did," I said, smiling.

On the way home I made some creepy animals on the
breezeway wall. Harry made some scary echoes to go
with them. He gave me some jelly beans and I gave
him some of my peppermint hippo.

"No thanks," he said. "Peppermint makes me sneeze."

And then I remembered Pansy's shampoo. It was
peppermint! No wonder Harry was always sneezing.

When we opened the door, Pansy was so happy to see Harry that she puddled.

The minute Harry saw Pansy, he sneezed.

"We're going to have to change your shampoo," I told Pansy.

Then, just as I was getting into bed again, Inky came into my room. "Tell me all about your walk with Harry," she said.

So I did.

When I was through, we did a one-minute barefoot ballet because it was late. "Now that things are settling down at our house," said Inky, kissing me good-night, "how about just you and me going out for the Kitchen Sink at Jan's tomorrow night?"

So on Saturday, Inky and I went out for ice cream.

But when we were leaving, Harry and Pansy looked so sad that we brought back a whole Kitchen Sink just for them.

When Inky, my mother, married Harry the shoe store man, there was music and dancing and cooking and tasting and talking and walking. Puddles to mop, sneezes to stop, and flip-flop shoes from Harry's store.

Inky lived with Harry, Harry lived with me, I lived with Inky, and we all lived together. "Isn't love the berries!" sang Harry.

"Once you get used to it," I sang.